THIS BOOK BELONGS TO

Welcome
is a
Wonderful Word

GYO FUJIKAWA

GROSSET & DUNLAP · PUBLISHERS · NEW YORK

A FILMWAYS COMPANY

Library of Congress Catalog Card Number: 80-81310. ISBN: 0-448-11748-7 (Trade Edition); ISBN: 0-448-13650-3 (Library Edition). Copyright © 1980 by Gyo Fujikawa.
All rights reserved. Published simultaneously in Canada. Printed in the United States of America.

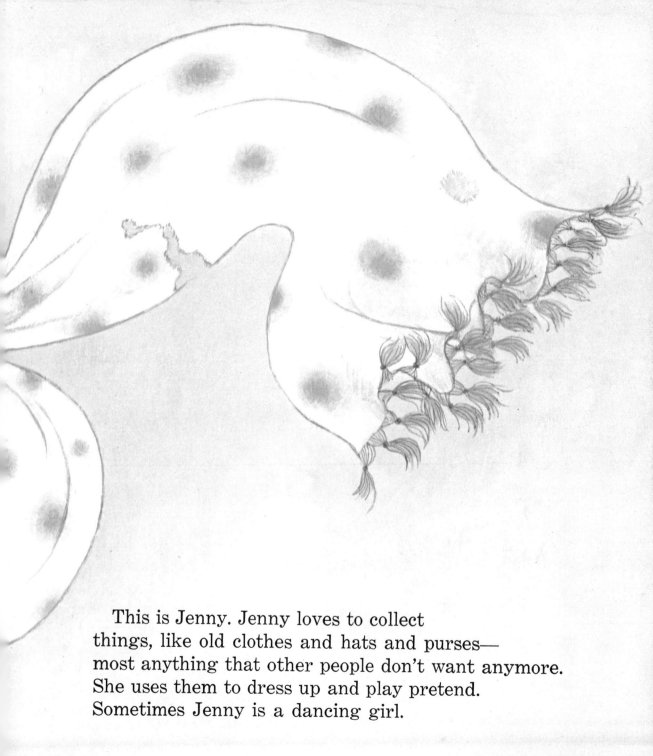

This is Jenny. Jenny loves to collect
things, like old clothes and hats and purses—
most anything that other people don't want anymore.
She uses them to dress up and play pretend.
Sometimes Jenny is a dancing girl.

Jenny knows everybody in the
neighborhood, and whenever she wants
more things, she goes from house
to house, collecting.

As soon as her shopping bag is full,
Jenny takes it to her playhouse.

There she shows her treasures
to her friends— Sam and Nicholas
and Sam's dog, Shags. They are
Jenny's very best friends.

All of them like
to play together.
They meet almost
every day at Jenny's
playhouse.

"Look what I got today!" Jenny said.
"Isn't this pretty?"

"Yes," Nicholas agreed, "but did you get
anything for me?"

"And for me?" Sam asked.

"Of course! Lots of things—for everybody!"
Jenny said happily.

Sometimes Nicholas is a doctor and Sam is a famous athlete. But no matter how hard he tries, Shags is always Shags.

Once Jenny gave a string of beads to
a friendly squirrel. But the squirrel thought
they were a little too big for him to wear.

One day Jenny said to her friends,
"You know the empty red house with the For Sale sign
in front? Well, it's not empty anymore. The sign's gone
and I saw smoke coming from the chimney."
"I wonder who's moved in," Sam said.
"That's what I mean to find out," Jenny said.

"I'm going to pick up some things from
Mrs. Brown," Jenny said. "And on the way back
I'll stop by the red house. I hope a little girl
lives there. It would be nice to have a new
friend. Then we'd be two boys and two girls."

Right after Jenny picked up the things from Mrs. Brown, she went to the red house. She saw somebody looking out the window. And sure enough, it was a little girl.

"Hello," Jenny called.

She went up
the walk toward the
house. All of a sudden
the little girl wasn't
at the window anymore.

Jenny walked to the
front door and knocked.
But nobody opened it.

So Jenny went to the window and looked
in. She was just in time to see the little
girl peeking around the curtain.

"Come out and play," Jenny called.
The little girl shook her head and
slipped away from the window.
"Why not?" Jenny asked.
But the little girl did not answer.

Jenny went back to where Sam and Nicholas and Shags were waiting. She told them about the new girl.

"She won't come out," Jenny said. "She won't be our new friend."

"I wonder why," Nicholas said.

Sam thought for a moment. "Maybe she doesn't feel welcome here."

"Then what should we do? How can we show her that we really want to be friends?" Jenny asked.

"I know," Sam cried. "I'll get my wagon and we'll fill it with things she might like!"

Jenny jumped up in the air.

"That's it!" she shouted.

"We'll make her feel welcome. We'll take her a welcome wagon!"

So Sam got his wagon and they piled it full of things.

Sam put in a baseball mitt and a football. Nicholas brought one of his favorite fishing rods and a little tin pail for worms. And Jenny packed up a scarf and beads, and best of all, a big hat with flowers.

Then they all hurried to the red house.

When they got there, they called to the little girl.

"Please come out!"
And Jenny shouted, "Come out and see what we have for you."
"We want to welcome you!" Nicholas added.

In a few minutes the door
opened and a shy little
girl stood there.

"What's your name?" Jenny asked.

"Mei Su," was the answer.

"Why don't you come out?"
Jenny asked.

"Because everybody gives you things,
and I don't know what to give you,"
Mei Su said.

"But you don't have to give me anything,"
Jenny said. "We want you to be our friend!"

So Mei Su came out.

And Jenny put the big hat with the big flowers on Mei Su's head. And Sam gave her the baseball mitt and the football. And Nicholas handed her the fishing pole.

"I'll show you how to play baseball," Sam said.

"And I'll show you how to catch a fish," Nicholas said.

"Oh, thank you," Mei Su exclaimed happily, with a big smile on her face. "Thank you so much!"

"Now we're all friends!" Jenny said.

"Let's have a cookie and lemonade party," Mei Su said.

And that afternoon Sam and Jenny
and Nicholas and Mei Su and Shags
did have a party.

When it was time for her friends to
go, Mei Su said, "I was sad when
I moved away from my old home. But
now I'm happy. You have made me
feel welcome."

"Welcome," Jenny said. "It's a
wonderful word, isn't it?"

"Yes," Nicholas agreed.

"The best," Sam said.

And Shags opened his mouth and
let out a loud and happy bark.